BORYA AND THE BURPS

An Eastern European Adoption Story

Joan McNamara

Illustrated by Dawn Majewski

Perspectives Press, Inc.
Indianapolis, Indiana

To Misha and her Godmother, Jackie, who have the best burps

For information address the publisher:
Perspectives Press, Inc.
P.O. Box 90318, Indianapolis, IN 46290-0318 (317) 872-3055
www.perspectivespress.com
Cover and interior design by Bookwrights
Manufactured in China

Library of Congress Cataloging-in-Publication Data

McNamara, Joan.
  Borya and the burps : an Eastern European adoption story / Joan McNamara ; illustrated by Dawn W. Majewski.
    p. cm.
  Summary: When baby Borya is adopted by a kind Mama-and-Papa, he leaves his Eastern European orphanage, taking nothing familiar with him except his talent for burping.
  ISBN 0-944934-31-5 (alk. paper)
  [1. Orphans—Fiction. 2. Babies—Fiction. 3. Adoption—Fiction. 4. Belching—Fiction. 5. Europe, Eastern—Fiction.] I. Majewski, Dawn, ill. II. Title.

PZ7.M232516Bo 2005
[E]—dc22   2004063518

Foreword for grownups reading Borya AND THE Burps!

When a family adopts a child from an orphanage, it is usually a long anticipated time of joy and excitement for parents. But the children being adopted often have other perceptions and feelings, from fearful to cheerful, from open to anxious. After all, this event called adoption involves moving from everything and everyone a child has ever known (no matter how deprived or how positive the environment) to go with strangers across a vast distance to an unknown place with unfamiliar food, language, and perhaps even an unfamiliar new name. It's no wonder that many children feel overstimulated and overwhelmed in the early days of adoption, and that some adopted children have shared that this positive event felt more like a kidnapping than a rescue to them at first.

To help children build strong and healthy attachments in their new families, parents need to learn as much as possible about the orphanage environment the children are coming from upon which the children's early experiences of security have been built. In part, these helpful insights make it much easier for new parents to learn to meet their children's needs consistently, build a sense of safe and secure structure in the new home, and ultimately help their child invest in and trust this new and loving forever family.

Joan

Borya was a little boy who lived with six other babies in white cribs, in a white room, in an orphanage. The room smelled like milk and blankets and diapers.

There were three boys in three white cribs on the right. There were three girls in three white cribs on the left. Borya was in a white crib in the middle.

The seven babies waved at each other through the bars of the seven white cribs.

Each day day the Mamachkas* came into the white room several times to help Borya and his friends in the white cribs drink milk from bottles, burp, and get diapers changed.

The Mamachkas knew that drinking a bottle of milk made milk bubbles inside that had to come out, or these would make a tummy ache.

So after each bottle the Mamachkas held each baby and patted the baby's back until a burp or two came out.

Then they smiled and said, "Good Baby!"

Borya always had the biggest, loudest, longest burp.

"Bu-r-r—P!" went Borya.

"Good Baby!" said the Mamachkas.

The Mamachkas smiled and Borya smiled too.

Borya liked that.

* Ma-Mach-ka: "Little mother" Sometimes nannies, nurses or caretakers at orphanages are called "Mama" or "Mamachka."

At night each of the seven babies was swaddled safe and tight and warm and tucked into a white crib for the night, with Borya in the middle.

During the night different Mamachkas came and kept watch in the white room with the seven babies in the seven white cribs.

Everything was quiet and still. Sometimes the oldest Mamachka would softly sing a song.

Borya liked that.

After the quiet sleep of night came morning again. This world was safe and familiar to each baby in the white room in the orphanage.

The babies in the seven white cribs knew that

- ✔ milk would always be there in bottles for them,
- ✔ Mamachkas would change diapers and pat backs to turn milk bubbles into burps,
- ✔ sometimes the oldest Mamachka would sing quietly at night,
- ✔ and Borya would always be in the middle, with three girls in cribs on the left and three boys in cribs on the right.

Borya liked that.

Borya and the other babies slept in seven white cribs in a white room in a place called an orphanage because their first parents could not be families for them. The seven babies were waiting for families, but they did not know this, because they were too little to understand.

The Mamachkas took care of the seven babies while other people looked and looked for forever families where the children could be loved and would grow up healthy and strong.

The Mamachkas would say, "Lucky Babies, you will have new Mamas and Papas soon."

But Borya and the other babies in the seven white cribs had never seen or heard or felt a Mama-and-Papa, so they didn't know what this meant.

There they were, in the white room that smelled like milk and blankets and diapers, content to drink their bottles, to wave their hands through the bars of their cribs, and to be burped.

One day, two new people came to the orphanage, to the white room with the seven white cribs with seven babies.

Borya, and even the Mamachkas, couldn't understand what the new people said.

One of the Mamachkas picked up the wiggly baby girl from a crib on the left to hand her to these strangers she called a "Mama-and-Papa."

There was lots of laughing and crying before the new people went away with the baby from the white crib on the left.

That night there were seven white cribs in the white room, but there were only six babies.

Borya was confused.

Where did our baby go?

Why did the Mama-and-Papa take her?

Why did the Mama-and-Papa talk funny?

Will the baby be all right?

What is a Mama-and-Papa?

Borya didn't feel like burping that night, and his tummy hurt.

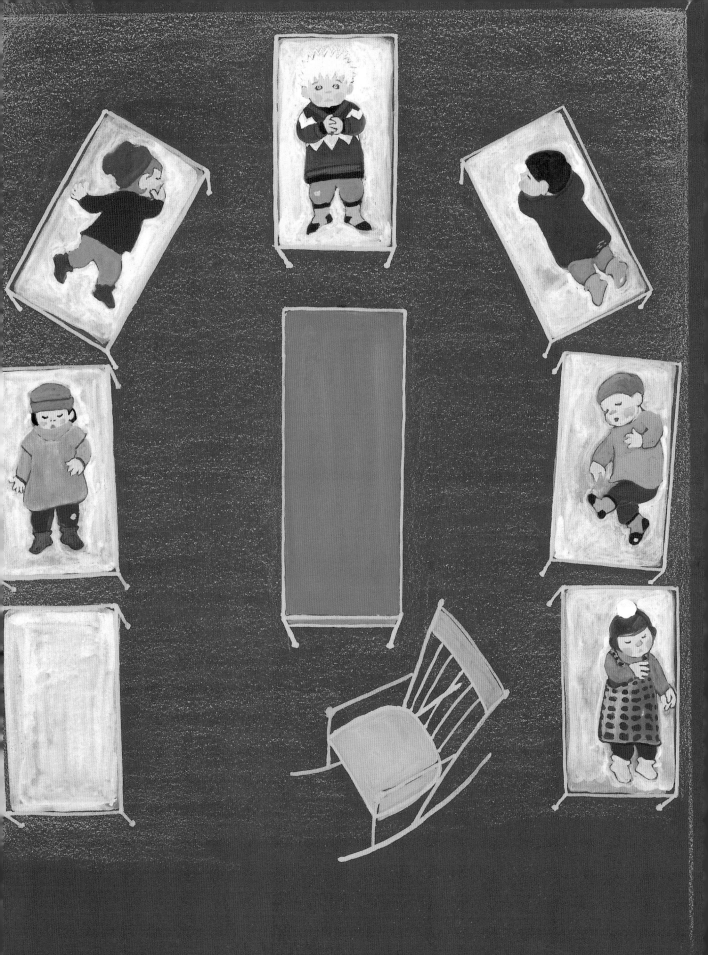

Days and nights later, another Mama-and-Papa came into the white room with seven white cribs.

Borya could tell they were a Mama-and-Papa because they were strangers who didn't speak right.

One of them had a pretty smile, like the Mamachkas, but the other one looked like the doctor-man who came to poke and prod the babies and sometimes stuck them with a needle.

Borya wondered, was this Mama-and-Papa going to stick Borya with a needle?

Borya wouldn't like that.

The Mamachka picked up Borya from his white crib in the middle, took him away from the other babies, and gave him to the Mama-and-Papa to hold. The Mama-and-Papa played peek-a-boo and Borya thought these people were funny.

The Mama-and-Papas were crying and smiling at the same time, which was very confusing to Borya.

The Mamachka said to the Mama-and-Papa, "This is your new boy! This is your son."

"This is your new Mama-and-Papa!" the Mamachka said to Borya, "Now you can all go Home together!"

Borya was confused again, and a little scared.

What is a Mama-and-Papa?

Why didn't these people talk right?

Where were they going?

And what was "Home"?

The Mama-and-Papa took Borya away from the white room that smelled of milk and blankets and diapers, away from the five other babies, and away from the Mamachkas.

They went into a street that was big and noisy, and then into a little car filled with bundles, and boxes, and bags, and bottles.

Borya had never been in such a big and noisy place. He had never been in a car.

Borya worried.

Where was his bottle? Who would feed him and help him burp?
Where were the Mamachkas? Who would diaper him and sing to him at night?
Where were his five friends in the white cribs in the white room?
Where was the smell of milk and blankets and diapers?
Where was his white crib? Where would he sleep?
And what was the place called "Home"?

Borya didn't like this.

The Mama-and-Papa drove with Borya to a big building, where they all went inside and walked into a crowded room with dark colors, many papers, and strange new people.

There were no white cribs, no Mamachkas, no smells of milk and blankets and diapers, and no singing.

At the front of the room, sat a stern woman, the Judge. She looked at them and at many papers, but there were no smiles.

Borya thought that maybe the judge had a tummy ache and couldn't burp.

Borya began to get hungry. One of the Mama-and Papas, the one with the pretty smile, had his bottle! Borya sat quietly on her lap and drank his bottle very fast, while everyone sat and sat in the crowded room with no smiles.

Though Borya could not understand them, the Mama-and-Papas said in soft whispers,

"The judge will write on the paper to say we can go Home with Borya, our new little boy."

They patted him gently on the back.

The judge looked at the Mama-and-Papas and she looked at Borya, and still she didn't smile, even when Borya finished his bottle all up.

And then, into the dusty quiet, one of the Mama-and-Papas, the one who looked like the doctor-man, gave a quiet little burp.

It was just a tiny, little one, not like Borya's nice big burps.

But the Mama-and-Papa turned red, and he looked at the judge, who frowned at him over the many papers.

Just then Borya, ready to get his milk bubbles up, gave his own burp.

"B-u-ur-r-P!", went Borya.

It was his longest, loudest burp yet.

All the people in the dark and sour room were even quieter. But the judge began to smile.

"Like father, like son!" the judge said, laughing.

She wrote on the papers to say that the Mama-and-Papas could go Home with their son, Borya.

The Mama-and-Papas smiled and cried and hugged.

Everyone smiled, but Borya was still confused.

The Mama-and-Papas scooped up Borya and ran out to the car filled with bundles, and boxes, and bags, and bottles. The bundles and boxes were left for the children at the orphanage, and the bags went with them as the car drove to a fat bus; the fat bus went to a busy train station; and the train chugged to a bustling airport.

The Mama-and-Papas, Borya and the bags boarded the airplane. They flew and flew through the day and night, to the new world for Borya called Home.

At Home, in a blue room with one blue crib, the Mama fed Borya a bottle and patted his back until he gave a small burp.

Then the Papa changed Borya's diaper, and wrapped him up snuggled in a new blue blanket, safe and tight and warm.

The Papa tucked Borya into the middle of a blue crib, with three teddy bears on the right and three teddy bears on the left.

The Mama sang a song to Borya until he fell asleep.

When Borya woke up, he was still at Home, in the blue room and in the middle of the blue crib, with three teddy bears on the right and three teddy bears on the left.

The room smelled like milk and blue blanket and teddy bears.

Papa picked Borya up and gave him his bottle, and Mama picked Borya up and patted his back softly.

Borya sat in the middle, between his Mama and his Papa.

And then Borya burped, "Bu-u-rr-rrp!"

It was the best and biggest burp ever, and everyone smiled.

About the Author

Joan McNamara, M.S., has been immersed in adoption for almost four decades as an adoptive parent, advocate and activist, and professional. Her research, training, and publications have been recognized and used widely in the US, Canada, the UK, and elsewhere around the world. But she says that it has been personal experiences with children in her own family and other families that have provided her with unique insights into some of the issues and thoughts of children coming from orphanages and foster care. Eleven of the thirteen children she and her husband Bernie have parented (now all adults) came into their family through adoption and foster care, many internationally.

Joan is now Education Coordinator for Carolina Adoption Services, Greensboro, N.C., and also founded and is Coordinator for the Home Again program at Carolina Adoption Services, currently the only organized program to assist children and families in crisis facing possible disruption of an international adoption. In addition, she is a member of the Education Committee of the Joint Council for International Children's Services.

Although there has been much written about international adoption for adults, there is far less from the perspectives of the children themselves, and no widely available materials for children related to Eastern European adoptions. Joan McNamara saw a need that desperately needed to be filled, and *Borya and the Burps* is her joyful and innovative contribution to the field, a loving gift to children from Eastern Europe and their new families

About the Publisher

Perspectives Press Inc
The Infertility and Adoption Publisher
www.perspectivespress.com

Since 1982 Perspectives Press, Inc has focused exclusively on infertility, adoption and related reproductive health and child welfare issues. Our purpose is to promote understanding of these issues and to educate and sensitize those personally experiencing these life situations, professionals who work in these fields, and the public at large. Our titles are never duplicative of or competitive with material already available through other publishers. We seek to find and fill niches which are empty.